Translated by Tara Chace.

First published in the United States and Canada in 2014 by NorthSouth Books Inc.,
an imprint of NordSüd Verlag AG, CH-8005, Zürich, Switzerland.

Distributed in the United States by NorthSouth Books Inc., New York 10016.
Library of Congress Cataloging-in-Publication Data is available.

ISBN: 978-0-7358-4184-0
Printed at Livonia Print, Latvia.
1 3 5 7 9 • 10 8 6 4 2
www.northsouth.com

FSC
www.fsc.org
MIX
Paper from
responsible sources
FSC® C104723

The Adventures of Pettson and Findus

Findus Disappears!

Sven Nordqvist

North
South

Old Man Pettson was working on his crossword puzzle when his cat Findus said, "Tell me about when I disappeared."

"You didn't disappear. You're sitting right here," Pettson said.

"I mean when I was little."

"But you already know that story."

"Tell it anyway. The whole story!" said the cat.

"All right," Pettson said, setting down his pencil. "The whole story it is . . ."

Once upon a time there was an old man named Pettson. He lived as comfortably as any old man could wish. The only trouble was, he sometimes felt lonely. He had neighbors, but they had their own lives. And of course he had his chickens; but whenever he was talking to them, they would suddenly run off because one of them had found a grub or something.

When it got dark, the little house often felt very empty and quiet. It was as if nothing was fun anymore.

One day Hattie Andersson from the farm next door stopped by to chat. She brought cinnamon rolls.

"You could use a wife to cheer you up," she said.

"No," Pettson replied. "I'm too old now. A whole woman—that would be too much. No, I don't need one."

"Why . . . you don't even have a cat."

"True," said Pettson. "Cats aren't that much trouble. Maybe I should get one."

The next week Hattie Andersson came back. This time she brought a cardboard box that said: "Findus Green Peas."

"What's this?" the old man asked. "The peas are squeaking."

He opened the box and there, on a piece of striped green cloth, stood a kitten. The kitten looked Pettson straight in the eye and squeaked.

"Hi, Findus Green Peas," Pettson said, and inside him it felt like someone had just opened the curtains on a summer morning and warm sunlight was streaming in.

"I'm Pettson, and this is my kitchen. You're going to live here now, if you want. Would you like some coffee?"

"He doesn't drink coffee," Hattie Andersson said. "Milk is what he wants."

Findus sank his claws into Pettson's finger and bit him.

"Ow, he bites," Pettson said with a smile. Then he looked worriedly at Old Lady Andersson. "Won't he miss his mother?"

"For a few days, maybe. Then he'll forget. You'll take care of him and be his new mother."

"Mother . . . ," Pettson repeated, happily watching as the kitten bit him. "Ow!"

The days were easier now. The house wasn't empty anymore. Pettson would leave Findus in the kitchen whenever he went out to chop some wood.

He'll be fine on his own for a bit, Pettson thought. *Cats can fend for themselves, everyone knows that. Although maybe I should go in and have another cup of coffee . . .*

He had never had so many cups of coffee in his life.

At last, Pettson had someone to talk to. He talked like he had never talked before. He told stories about his childhood—about cows he'd known, about how potatoes grew, yes, about anything that came into his head. He thought it was a shame that Findus couldn't say anything back. Findus just squeaked. Pettson thought, *If I talk enough maybe he'll learn how.*

Every night Pettson read fairy tales to Findus. Well, not always fairy tales. Sometimes it was an article about a new combine harvester or a short story from a magazine about a nurse who'd fallen in love.

Findus sat quietly in his lap and listened, looking at the pictures, if there were any.

And then one day, Findus looked for a long time at a picture of a clown in big, striped pants.

"I want pants like that," Findus said.

Pettson stared at him. These were the cat's first words.

"Then you'll have some," the old man said. "I'll sew you a pair right away."

He smiled happily as he got out his sewing box.
What a cat he had!

The weeks passed. Findus got bigger. Now he ran around on his own however he pleased. When they had to go a little farther, all the way to the carpentry shed, for example, he would sit on Pettson's shoulder. Findus wanted to be with him everywhere. He talked nonstop. The quiet, empty house was full of talking and running.

Every morning Findus woke Pettson up by jumping on him or wrestling with his big toe. Just the thought of living alone again made the old man sad, so he quickly stopped thinking about it. And why should he when the little cat in his big trousers was bouncing up and down on his belly, yelling, "Wake up, Pettson! Time to play!"

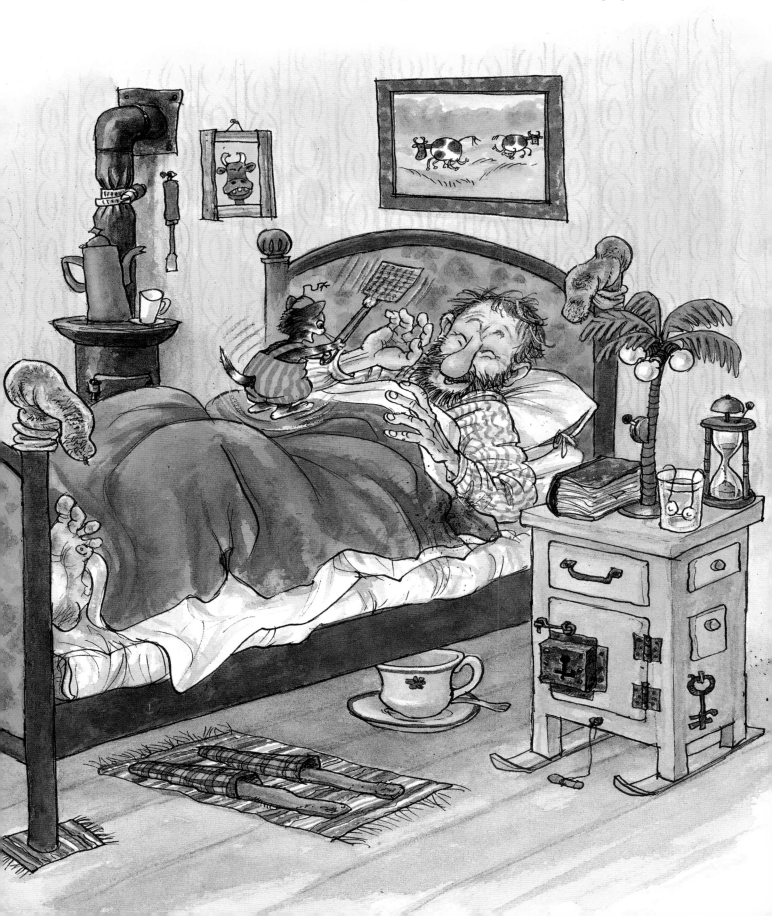

But one morning Pettson
woke up because he felt
something was wrong. The
house was silent and there
was no cat to wake him.

"Findus, where are you?"
he cried, looking under the
covers, under the bed, and
inside his shoes. He looked
and yelled everywhere.
Barefoot, he ran out to the
toolshed, and the woodshed,
and the chicken coop.

He flung open the door, sending the chickens flying.

The hens clucked, "Help, a thief!" "Pettson's not wearing any pants!"

"Quiet!" Pettson yelled. "Findus is missing. Have you seen him?"

"Nope. Buck-buck-buck-gock! Not today anyway," clucked Giddy. "Say, aren't you the guy who takes our eggs?"

Those chickens never knew what was happening. And Pettson himself didn't know that his little cat was sitting just ten yards away, terrified for his life.

Findus had gone exploring in the house while Pettson was still sleeping.

He discovered the world of mice and small creepy crawly things. This is where they lived and kept all the items Pettson lost.

Findus made his way through the walls and down narrow passages. Then suddenly he was blinded by sunlight streaming in through some gaps in the house's foundation.

He emerged into the tall grass outside the house. He didn't know where he was.

Then he heard something rustling and grunting in the grass—something big. He turned around and saw a large furry blob coming straight toward him.

Every single hair on Findus rose in terror. Like a steel spring, he jumped into the scrap heap, landing inside an old box.

He saw the dreadful beast through a knothole. It was making a bunch of noise, as if it was talking to itself. *It's searching for kittens to eat*, Findus thought.

He sat as quietly as he could and hoped that the beast wouldn't discover him.

Then he heard Pettson calling! But he didn't dare yell back, because the beast might find him.

The minutes passed and the gray lump of fur was still right outside the box. Findus started crying.

"There's a lot of crying going on in here," a voice said.

Findus saw two of those small animals that lived in the house. He called them "mumbles."

"There's a terrible animal out there who's planning to eat me up!" Findus sobbed.

"Oh dear, oh dear," said one of the mumbles. "I suppose you'd better stay here."

"I can tell you stories," the other said.

"I can tell even better ones," said the first mumble.

"Once upon a time . . ."

The story was about a mumble who found a cat in a box. But mostly it was about how clever the mumble was, with almost nothing about the poor cat.

"Can't you go tell Pettson I'm here?" Findus cried.

"That would be very difficult. He doesn't speak our language. He doesn't even see us."

"Yeah, he's a little dim," the other mumble said. "But we could give him a few hints. We'll fix this. We fixinate everything!"

Findus felt better already.

Pettson searched the whole house again. He was really worried now.

He decided to get dressed properly, but he couldn't find his socks or his shoes. It was always like this! Things just disappeared, and then he would find them much later somewhere else. As if there was someone in the house who borrowed his things.

But no matter how much he scratched his head or tugged on his beard, it didn't help. His shoes and socks were gone, just like Findus.

He put on his boots and went outside to search. But here were his shoes—right in front of the house, as if they had walked out on their own. Then he spotted his socks, stretched out like arrows.

He followed the arrows until he saw the old badger, who liked to sniff around at dusk.

"Hi, badger," Pettson said.

The badger saw the old man, then quickly waddled up the hill.

"Findus!" Pettson yelled. "Are you out here?!"

"Yeeeeesssss! Here I am!" And there, in a damp old wooden box, stood little Findus jumping for joy!

Pettson picked him up and the cat clung to his neck.

"Oh, Pettson," he whimpered. "You saved me from that terrible beast. Take me home! It's dangerous here."

"No it's not," Pettson said. "That was just the old badger. It doesn't eat cats. If you don't bother it, then it won't bother you. You would do better to find all the hiding spots now so you'll know where to go if a fox or some silly dog comes by."

Findus looked around, still terrified. Then finally he dared to get down on the ground.

He explored everything, and every once in a while his head would pop up somewhere and he'd call, "Hi, Pettson!"

The old man sat by while the cat got to know every single nook.

They went back inside and had breakfast. Pettson asked about the shoes and socks that had shown him the way.

"No, I didn't put them there," Findus said. "The mumbles did that. They're my friends. They live here too."

"Oh, I see," said Pettson. "If you say so. Then I suppose I won't ever need to feel lonely again. Since I have neighbors and chickens and mumbles. And this little cat.

"Then . . . well, then they lived happily every after," Pettson said, finishing his story.

Findus smiled contentedly.

"That little cat, that's me," he said.

"Yes it is," the old man replied. "You're lucky I found you before the badger ate you up."

"Oh, he's not dangerous," Findus said. "We're friends now. He's nice."

"You can make friends with anyone."

"Yes," said the cat, thinking. "But you're my best friend."

"Hmm," the old man said, and smiled. "Likewise."

Findus Disappears!

Cast of Characters

Findus is Pettson's clever, curious, and affectionate cat. He's always up for an adventure and meets new friends along the way.

Pettson is Findus's patient and loving owner—a smart and forgetful farmer and inventor.

Hattie Anderson is Pettson's doting next-door neighbor. She's a great baker and is the reason that Findus and Pettson met!

The chickens don't need much of an introduction. These feathered fowl are always on the scene but rarely know what's going on.

The mumbles are the friendly little creatures that "borrow" Pettson's things. Pettson can't see them, but Findus can.

Old badger is a grumbling, snorting creature, but he means no harm. Soon, he and Findus are good friends.

Sven Nordqvist is the author and illustrator who dreamed up this series. The beloved Pettson and Findus stories draw on Nordqvist's playful adventures with his two sons when they were younger. His unique illustrations are inspired by the delights of everyday life.